FRAN
WORLD
OOPS
DAD FACTS
BEWARE OF DOG

YEAH
OOPS

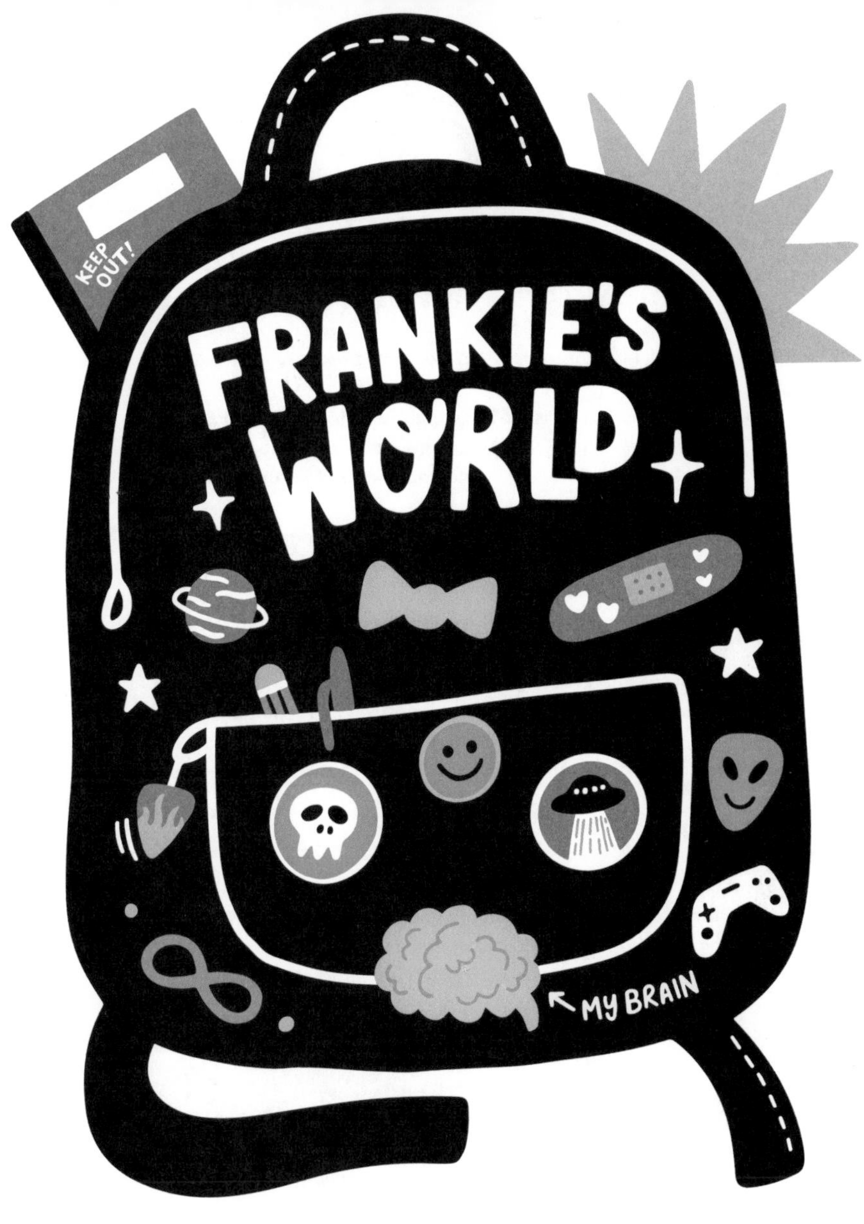

FRANKIE'S WORLD

AOIFE DOOLEY

An Imprint of
SCHOLASTIC

First published in the United Kingdom in 2022 by Scholastic UK.

Library of Congress Control Number: 2021948451

ISBN 978-1-338-81312-8 (hardcover)
ISBN 978-1-338-81311-1 (paperback)

10 9 8 7 6 5 4 3 2 1 22 23 24 25 26

Printed in the U.S.A. 40
This edition first printing, August 2022

For anyone and everyone who
feels like they don't fit in

NAME: FRANKIE

AGE: 11 YEARS OLD

HEIGHT: SMALLEST IN MY CLASS

THINGS I LOVE: ART, PIZZA, AND ROCK MUSIC

THINGS I DON'T LOVE: SCHOOL, THE HOSPITAL, AND POP MUSIC

CHAPTER 1

WELCOME TO MY WORLD

HI, I'M FRANKIE! SOMETHING YOU SHOULD KNOW ABOUT ME IS I TALK TOO MUCH.

I JUST
yap!
YAP
YAP!
YAP
yap!
SPRIN

CAN'T

HELP IT!

I ALWAYS SAY THE WRONG THING AT THE WORST TIME.
DID YOU KNOW THAT SOME TURTLES CAN BREATHE OUT OF THEIR BUTTS?
RIP
PICKLES

WHO'S MY CELEBRITY LOOK-ALIKE?
BUZZ LIGHTYEAR!

WHOA! THEY'RE SOME BIG FEET! I BET WHEN YOU KICK A SOCCER BALL, IT GOES FOR MILES.

BUT BESIDES THAT, I'M DEFINITELY THE COOLEST PERSON I KNOW.
HOW I THINK PEOPLE SEE ME
PURE GENUS GENIUS
COOLEST IN CLASS
NOT AFRAID OF ANYTHING (EVEN SPIDERS)
ABSOLUTE LEGEND
WELL, KIND OF...
HOW PEOPLE ACTUALLY SEE ME
LOSER
AFRAID OF ABSOLUTELY EVERYTHING

I'M A BIT DIFFERENT FROM OTHERS IN MY CLASS.
SPORTY
GIRLY
7

I'M THE ONLY ONE WHO LIKES ROCK MUSIC, FOR A START. EVERYONE ELSE LISTENS TO POP MUSIC, WHICH ISN'T NEARLY AS GOOD.
IDLES
THE BEST
F

I TRY TO BLEND IN FOR THE MOST PART, BECAUSE I HAVE ENOUGH TO WORRY ABOUT AS IT IS. TRUST ME!

EVERY MONTH, I HAVE TO GO TO THE DOCTOR TO MAKE SURE I'M GROWING.
THE DOCTOR SAID I'M WAY TOO SMALL FOR MY AGE.
THE ONLY GOOD THING IS I GET TO MISS SCHOOL FOR A COUPLE OF HOURS.
WOODVILLE SCHOOL
DOCTOR MORAN IS NICE BUT HE ASKS TOO MANY QUESTIONS. MORE THAN ME, EVEN.
DO YOU LIKE DOGS?
HOW'S SCHOOL?
HOW ARE YOU FEELING?
O Z
P E D

WHEN PEOPLE ASK HOW I'M FEELING, I NEVER KNOW WHAT TO SAY. HOW AM I SUPPOSED TO KNOW? PRINCIPAL DALY ASKS ME ALL THE TIME. SHE EVEN GAVE ME THIS JOURNAL.
MEH
FRANKIE
KEEP OUT!
BORING
MATH

SHE DIDN'T GIVE ONE TO ANYONE ELSE. WHAT'S SO SPECIAL ABOUT ME? I BET IT'S THIS NEW FRECKLE I'VE GOT!
WHAT THE!

I JUST WOKE UP ONE MORNING AND THERE IT WAS, RIGHT IN THE MIDDLE OF MY FACE.

ALL I KNOW IS, SINCE IT POPPED UP, PRINCIPAL DALY HAS BEEN HAVING MEETINGS WITH MAM ALMOST EVERY DAY.
PE DAY

THEY ALWAYS GIVE ME A FUNNY LOOK. THIS ONE RIGHT HERE!

MAYBE THEY'RE THINKING OF REMOVING MY FRECKLE AND PUTTING IT IN A MUSEUM...
WOW!
IT'S SO FAMOUS, IT EVEN HAS ITS OWN NETFLIX SERIES. SEASON 7 IS COMING THIS SPRING!
DO NOT TOUCH

PEOPLE IN MY CLASS GIVE ME LOOKS, TOO. SOMETIMES THEY SAY MEAN THINGS.
HA HA!
STUPID
UGLY
FREAK
WEIRDO

EXCEPT MY BEST FRIEND, SAM.

SHE THINKS I'M SOME SORT OF ALIEN. I HOPE I AM, BECAUSE IT WOULD EXPLAIN A LOT!
LOADING...
99%
GREETINGS

I'D JUST HOP INTO MY SPACESHIP, BLAST OFF, AND NEVER HAVE TO DEAL WITH ANYONE EVER AGAIN!
HOME AT LAST

ONE PERSON I'D LIKE TO NEVER SEE AGAIN IS MS. CRACKLE, MY TEACHER. SHE'S SCARY! HER SKIN LOOKS LIKE A RAISIN, AND HER BREATH SMELLS LIKE A BIN FULL OF ROTTEN CABBAGES. I'VE NO IDEA WHAT THAT SMELLS LIKE, BUT I'M GUESSING IT'S PRETTY BAD.

MS. CRACKLE

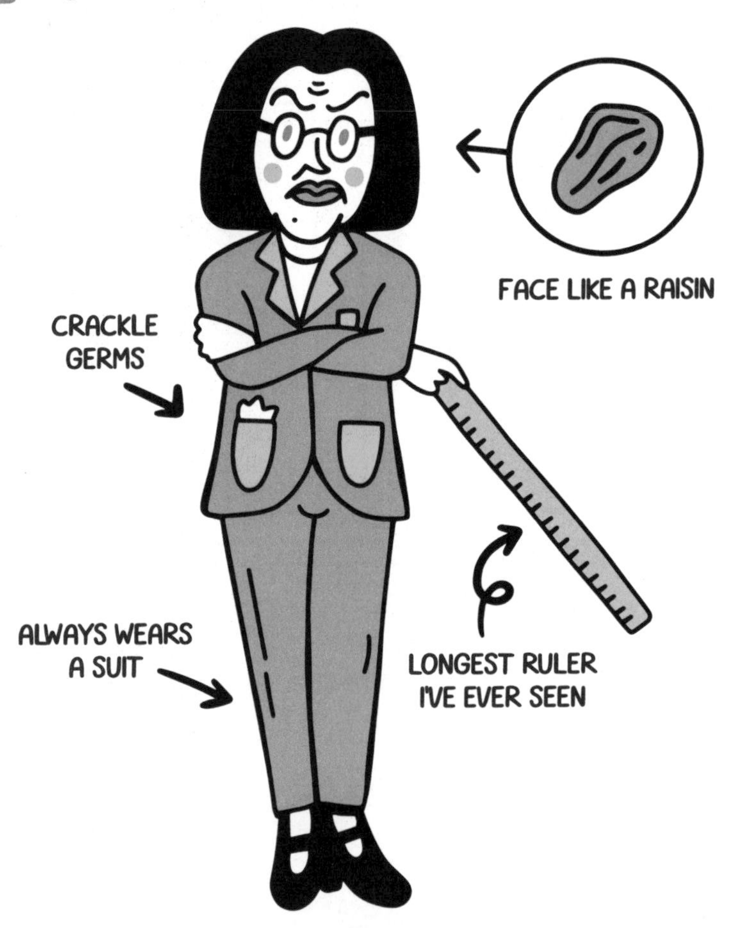

MS. CRACKLE HAS THIS DRAWER, AND INSIDE THERE'S AN OLD BOW TIE. SHE USES IT AS PUNISHMENT FOR ANY BOYS OR GIRLS WHO FORGET THEIRS.

AND IT'S NOT JUST ANY BOW TIE...
THE HAUNTED BOW TIE
OLDER THAN YOUR GRANDAD
DRIED-ON SNOT

I HEARD ONE GIRL'S HEAD SPUN AROUND FIVE TIMES AFTER PUTTING IT ON. SHE EVEN HAD TO LEAVE THE SCHOOL!

NOBODY KNOWS WHO THE ORIGINAL OWNER IS. SOME SAY IT'S CRACKLE HERSELF! IT MIGHT BE – THEY'RE PROBABLY THE SAME AGE.
CRACKLE IN THE WILD

MAYBE IF I WEAR IT I'LL GET TO LEAVE SCHOOL, TOO. I COULD BRING IN FAKE BLOOD TO MAKE IT REALLY CONVINCING...
AHH!
AHH!

THAT WOULD BE A GREAT PLAN IF MY MAM DIDN'T CHECK EVERY MORNING, WITHOUT FAIL, THAT I'M WEARING MINE.
NO!
NO
NO!
No

ANYWAY, BACK TO CRACKLE.

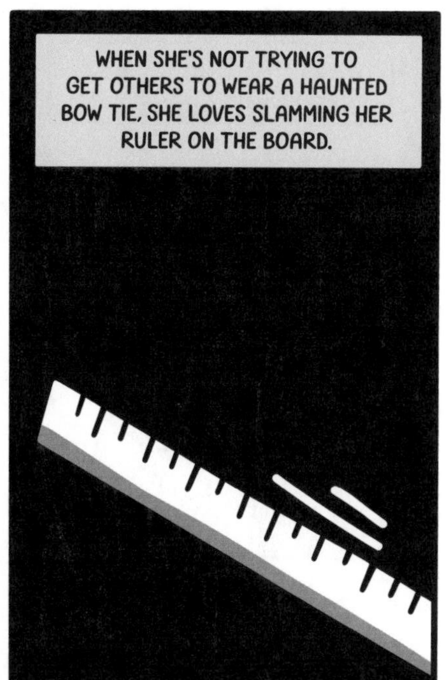
WHEN SHE'S NOT TRYING TO GET OTHERS TO WEAR A HAUNTED BOW TIE, SHE LOVES SLAMMING HER RULER ON THE BOARD.

SLAM!

THE NOISE MAKES MY BRAIN FEEL LIKE IT'S GOING TO EXPLODE.

EVERY TIME IT HAPPENS, I CAN HEAR REBECCA GASPING AS IF SHE'S JUST RUN A MARATHON.
PUFF
PUFF

AND IT MAKES PAUL SHAKE LIKE A LEAF! BUT THEN AGAIN, HE'S AFRAID OF EVERYTHING.
AHH!

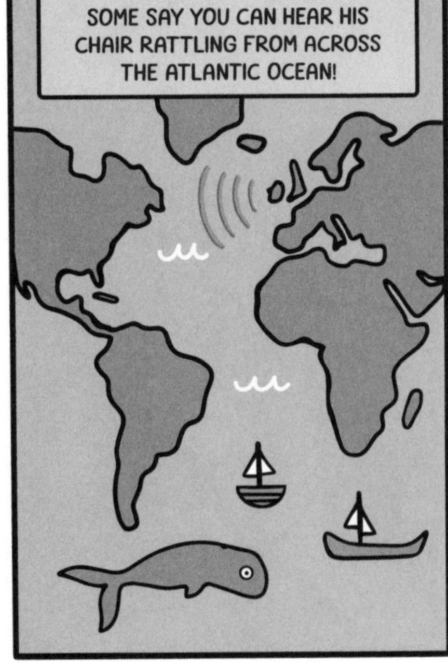
SOME SAY YOU CAN HEAR HIS CHAIR RATTLING FROM ACROSS THE ATLANTIC OCEAN!

NADINE AND SHAUNA ARE IN MY CLASS, TOO. THERE'S ONLY THREE THINGS YOU NEED TO KNOW ABOUT THEM.

(1) THEY'RE REALLY MEAN
(2) THEY'RE TOUGHER THAN THEY LOOK
(3) THEY THINK LOOKING GOOD IS THE MOST IMPORTANT THING

THREE DAYS AGO, THEY TOOK SAM'S NEW SNEAKERS FOR NO REASON! WHO DOES THAT?

NADINE'S FISTS ARE ABOUT THE SAME SIZE AS A BUNCH OF BANANAS. THEY DON'T FEEL LIKE BANANAS, THOUGH...

ONCE, SHE HIT ME SO HARD I HAD A BRUISE FOR NEARLY A YEAR. I EVEN HAD IT IN MY SCHOOL PICTURE.

HER MAM IS JUST AS MEAN, AND SHE ALWAYS HAS THIS WEIRD BANDAGE ON HER NOSE. IT MAKES HER LOOK LIKE AN ANCIENT MUMMY!
BYE, SWEETIE! REMEMBER TO SUCK THAT BELLY IN!

SAM SAID IT'S TO HOLD EVERYTHING TOGETHER BECAUSE SHE'S OLD. I DON'T KNOW IF SHE WAS JOKING, THOUGH.

SOMETIMES I LIKE TO PRETEND I'M SOMEWHERE ELSE. LIKE A HOLIDAY FOR MY BRAIN!

SOMEWHERE WITH ALL MY FAVORITE FOOD...
AHHH! THIS IS NICE.
MISS! YOUR DINNER IS READY!

BUT FOR NOW, I'M STUCK IN THIS DUMP.
FRANKIE!

LUNCHTIME IS OK. SAM AND I USUALLY PLAY BASKETBALL.
PASS! I'M OPEN!
THERE'S ONLY TWO OF US PLAYING, YOU HAM!

WHENEVER WE'RE HANGING OUT WITH ANYONE ELSE, WE'RE ALWAYS PICKED LAST, SO USUALLY WE DON'T BOTHER.
I PICK SHAUNA!
PAUL.
NADINE.

MAM THINKS IT'S BECAUSE I HURT PEOPLE'S FEELINGS (YOU KNOW, BECAUSE I ALWAYS SAY THE WRONG THING).

DID YOU KNOW: MONKEYS IN JAPAN ARE SO SMART, THEY KNOW HOW TO USE VENDING MACHINES? I DON'T EVEN KNOW HOW TO USE MY OWN BRAIN!

IT'S LIKE MY BRAIN HAS ALL THESE TINY LITTLE PEOPLE INSIDE.
FULL OF FEELINGS
WORDS

EACH WITH THEIR OWN JOB TO DO.
IN CHARGE OF THOUGHTS
IN CHARGE OF FEELINGS
IN CHARGE OF SPEECH

I LOOOVE THIS SHOW!
PULL TO SAY SOMETHING RANDOM
BUT SOME OF THEM MAKE ME SAY AND DO THE WRONG THINGS AND GET ME INTO TROUBLE.

SAM'S BRAIN IS THE COMPLETE OPPOSITE.
I DID IT!
BRAIN SCHOOL
SAM, TELL US WHAT THE ANSWER IS.
THE ANSWER IS TWELVE, MS. CRACKLE!
SHE'S THE SMARTEST IN OUR CLASS.

IN MY HOUSE, THERE'S ME;
MY SISTER, ABBEY, WHO IS SIX;
MAM; AND MY STEPDAD, JERRY.

ALL ABBEY DOES IS EAT, SLEEP, MOAN, AND GIVE ME A HEADACHE. SHE'S ONLY EVER NICE TO ME ON MY BIRTHDAY BECAUSE THERE'S CAKE.
BLEHHH!

JERRY WORKS NIGHT SHIFTS SO I DON'T REALLY SEE HIM DURING THE DAY. I THINK HE MIGHT BE HALF VAMPIRE!
WHY DOES THE KITCHEN STINK OF GARLIC? I HATE GARLIC.

MY MAM IS MY OTHER BEST FRIEND.

I WISH WE COULD DO MORE TOGETHER, LIKE SAM AND HER MAM.

MY MAM'S HEART DOESN'T BEAT RIGHT, SO SHE HAS TO GO TO THE DOCTOR FOR CHECK-UPS ALL THE TIME.

SOMETIMES I WORRY ABOUT HER, BUT EVEN WHEN SHE'S HAVING A BAD DAY, SHE'S STILL ALWAYS SMILING.

MY HOUSE IS SMALL. WE'RE NOT RICH, BUT SOMEDAY I WILL BE. THEN I'LL BUY A MANSION!
I LIVE HERE

IT WILL HAVE A POOL, A GAME ROOM FOR ME AND SAM, A CHEF TO MAKE FOOD 24/7, AND MY ROOM WOULD BE BIGGER THAN THE SCHOOL!

OH! AND SEVEN TOILETS, BECAUSE THEN NO ONE WOULD BE BANGING THE DOOR DOWN EVERY TWO MINUTES!
FRANKIE! ARE YOU STILL IN THERE?
FINISHED, MAM!
KEEP OUT

I WOULDN'T CHANGE ANYTHING ABOUT MY ROOM, THOUGH. I LOVE IT!
I BELIEVE
IDLES
PUNK

CHAPTER 2

THE NEXT DAY
WHEN DO I GET TO STOP GOING HERE?

I DON'T KNOW, SWEETHEART. HOPEFULLY WE'LL KNOW MORE AFTER THIS APPOINTMENT.
THAT'S WHAT YOU SAID THE LAST TIME.

THE HOSPITAL IS MY SECOND LEAST FAVORITE PLACE.
HOSPITAL
AMBULANCE

IT SMELLS FUNKY AND YOU HAVE TO SIT AROUND FOR HOURS. IT'S SO DULL.

HI, FRANKIE, WOULD YOU LIKE TO COME IN?
FINALLY...

WOW! YOU'VE GROWN SO BIG! THAT'S GREAT! YOU MUST BE EATING ALL YOUR VEGETABLES.
ALL I EAT IS WAFFLES.

WELL, GREAT PROGRESS THIS MONTH. DOCTOR MORAN WILL BE IMPRESSED! HERE, HAVE A STICKER.
I WAS BRAVE TODAY

HERE WE GO AGAIN...
HEY, FRANKIE! HOW IS SCHOOL GOING? YOU'RE STARTING SEVENTH GRADE NEXT YEAR! HOW IS YOUR FRIEND SAM?
. . .
. . .
. . .
. . .
. . .

DOESN'T THIS GUY KNOW HOW TO TAKE A BREATH?
MY FILES
FRANKIE

NOW I HAVE SOME GOOD NEWS, AND I HAVE SOME BAD NEWS.

THE GOOD NEWS IS YOU'RE GROWING. THE BAD NEWS IS...NOT FAST ENOUGH.

WHAT DOES THAT MEAN?

I'M GOING TO PRESCRIBE A GROWTH HORMONE THAT WILL HOPEFULLY SPEED THINGS UP.

Ha
YOU'LL HAVE TO GET AN INJECTION ON YOUR BUM, BUT JUST ONCE A MONTH.
GREAT, THIS IS ALL I NEED.
FASHION

WHY DON'T I FIT IN, MAM?
YOU WILL! I PROMISE.

BUT WHAT IF I NEVER DO?

WHAT IF SOMETHING IS SERIOUSLY WRONG?
HAVE A GREAT DAY, SWEETIE!

IN SCHOOL
MATH
YOU'RE LATE AGAIN, FRANKIE!

I CAN'T TELL CRACKLE WHY I WAS ABSENT NOW! I DON'T WANT EVERYONE TO FIND OUT I WAS AT THE HOSPITAL.

PSSST, FRANKIE!

TEACHER TEACHER!
FRANKIE HAS A NOTE

WELL, WHAT COULD BE MORE IMPORTANT THAN MATH?
ENGLISH?

THAT WASN'T A QUESTION, YOU SILLY GIRL! GO TO PRINCIPAL DALY.

PRINCIPAL

I THINK YOU'LL BE ABLE TO CONCENTRATE BETTER IN HERE. IT WILL BE FUN! NO DISTRACTIONS.
BUT, PRINCIPAL DALY, I DIDN'T EVEN DO ANYTHING! IT WAS...

I'LL BE BACK IN FIVE MINUTES.

EWW! THIS IS DEFINITELY A DISTRACTION, AND NOT A GOOD ONE!

SO GROSS!

WHAT'S THIS?
NADINE

NADINE
NOT APPLYING HERSELF - MAY HAVE TO REPEAT 6TH GRADE IF SHE DOESN'T IMPROVE.
GRADE D
MIXING WITH PEERS

OMG!

SOMEONE IS COMING!!!

SORRY I
TOOK SO LONG!
THAT WAS CLOSE.

LUNCHTIME
AND THEN THERE WAS A PICTURE LIKE THIS...

AND THEN WHAT HAPPENED?

OH!

WHAT THE??
YEAH! I SAW IT WITH MY OWN EYES.

ARE YOU SERIOUS?
DO YOU KNOW WHAT
THIS MEANS?!

WHAT ARE YOU TWO
TALKING ABOUT?

DID YOU
KNOW THAT —
THAT FRANKIE'S A FREAK?
EVERYONE KNOWS. IT EVEN RHYMES.
FRANKIE THE FREAK!

THAT'S ACTUALLY NOT A RHYME. IT'S CALLED ALLITERATION.

EWW, FRANKIE FARTED! IT SMELLS LIKE MOLDY BEANS.

WHY ARE THE MOST ANNOYING PEOPLE IN OUR CLASS?
BECAUSE WE'RE THE UNLUCKIEST PEOPLE ON THE PLANET, REMEMBER?

DING! DING!

ART
COMPETITION
YAY!
YAY!
YAY!
ART IS MY FAVORITE CLASS. IT'S THE ONLY THING I'M REALLY GOOD AT. MS. JONES IS THE BEST TEACHER EVER!
I'VE GOT SOME EXCITING NEWS! IN TWO WEEKS, WE HAVE AN ART COMPETITION.

YEEEESSS! I'M GOING TO DRAW AN ALIEN EATING A HOT DOG.

THE THEME IS YOUR TRUE SELF. THERE WILL BE FIRST, SECOND, AND THIRD PLACE.
NEVER MIND.

HOW WAS SCHOOL? DID YOU LEARN ANYTHING NEW?
MEH. IT WAS BORING, AS USUAL.

WELL, I'VE GOT A SURPRISE FOR YOU AT HOME.
DO I GET A SURPRISE, TOO?

IS IT A PUPPY? A GUITAR? A PHONE?
NO, AND ABBEY, STOP KICKING THE CHAIR!

BACKSTAGE PASSES! A HELICOPTER RIDE TO A CONCERT? A LIMO?
VIP

IS IT AAAAA NEW POSTER? A HAMSTER?

9
11
WILL YOU EVER BE QUIET! ALL YOU DO IS TALK!
IS IT A...

IN MY HOUSE, WE DON'T EAT DINNER AT THE TABLE.

BUT I DON'T MIND BECAUSE WE GET TO WATCH TV.
HA HA

MAM! MY CHICKEN IS TOUCHING THE SAUCE AGAIN.
IT'S ALL GOING TO BE TOUCHING WHEN IT'S IN YOUR TUMMY, FRANKIE.

BUT I HATE WHEN MY FOOD TOUCHES, IT'S GROSS.
IT'S FINE, DON'T BE SO SENSITIVE.

I ATE ALL MINE, MAM. CAN I HAVE FRANKIE'S PRESENT NOW?

FRANKIE!

GAME OVER
OUT
EVERYONE ALWAYS SAYS I'M TOO SENSITIVE. I NEED TO GET TOUGH, AND FAST!

I'M NOT AFRAID OF ANYTHING!

GIANT SPIDER
BOOP!

AHH!
AHH!

AND IT WAS THIS SIZE! AND IT NEARLY TOUCHED MY TOE...BUT THEN IT DIDN'T.

ARE YOU READY FOR YOUR SURPRISE NOW?

TA-DA!

HOME
WHAT THE...? BUT I DON'T DO KARATE!
WELL, YOU DO NOW! IT'S TIME YOU LEARNED HOW TO STAND UP FOR YOURSELF. I KNOW YOU'VE BEEN HAVING A HARD TIME IN SCHOOL.

WHEN I SAID I NEEDED TO GET TOUGH, THIS IS NOT WHAT I HAD IN MIND.

BUT, MAM, I DON'T KNOW ANYONE THERE! WHAT IF SOMEONE BEATS ME UP? WHAT IF SOMEONE...

WHAT IF IT'S FUN?

IF YOU THINK THAT'S FUN, THEN YOU DON'T KNOW WHAT *FUN* IS.

EATING ICE CREAM IS FUN. PLAYING COMPUTER GAMES, FUN!

YOU'RE GOING, FRANKIE. AND THAT'S THAT.
NO, I'M NOT!!

WHY DO I HAVE TO GO TO THIS THING? IF I WANT TO GET BEATEN UP, ALL I HAVE TO DO IS LOOK AT NADINE.

TRAVEL
PIZZA
FASHUN
BAKERY
COFFEE
SHOP
I DON'T NEED TO PAY FOR IT.

DOJO
THIS IS THE WORST SURPRISE EVER.

WELCOME TO THE CLASS! WHAT'S YOUR NAME?
FRANKIE.

EVERYONE HERE SEEMS TO BE WEIRD AND GOOFY, TOO. NO ONE HAS FISTS LIKE BANANA BUNCHES, SO I THINK I'LL BE OK.

AND THEN WE LEARNED THIS MOVE
AND THIS MOVE AND THIS MOVE.
AND THEN WE SPARRED!

THAT'S ANOTHER
WORD FOR FIGHTING,
YOU KNOW!

SO YOU ENJOYED
YOURSELF? YOU COULD
EVEN SAY, HAD FUN.

CHAPTER 3

MY DAD'S AN ALIEN!

WELL, I GOT MY FIRST INJECTION. ALL I'M SAYING IS I BETTER GROW NOW.

EARLIER THAT DAY...
YOU WON'T FEEL A THING! NOW TAKE A DEEP BREATH FOR ME.

I HAVE TO WEAR THIS BANDAGE. AT LEAST NO ONE CAN SEE IT!
EWW, SO GIRLY!

I STILL HAVEN'T FIGURED OUT WHAT I'M DOING FOR THE ART COMPETITION, EITHER.

HOW AM I SUPPOSED TO CREATE SOMETHING FOR IT WHEN I DON'T EVEN KNOW MY "TRUE SELF"?
FRANKIE, CAN YOU GO TO THE SHOP FOR ME? WE NEED SOME BREAD.

OH YEAH
WHOO
I WON
WHOO

ON THE WAY TO THE SHOP
I'M GOING TO USE YELLOW, GREEN, AND BLUE. WHAT ARE YOU GOING TO DRAW?
I DON'T KNOW YET...

BUT THE COMPETITION IS ONLY A WEEK AWAY! YOU HAVE TO THINK OF SOMETHING!

SAM MIGHT BE SMART, BUT SHE'S JUST AS CLUELESS ABOUT READING BODY LANGUAGE AS I AM.
YAP
YAP

BRAIN LICKERS! DID YOUR MAM GIVE YOU EXTRA FOR SWEETS?
WELL, BREAD DOESN'T COST THAT MUCH, SO...
- BRAIN LICKER -

Lotto
ID
18
AND I'LL HAVE THE BIG BAG OF JELLIES, BRAIN LICKERS, GUMMY BEARS, CHOCOLATE COINS...

06
-PAT'S SHOP-
06
SO MAYBE WE HAVE TO FIGURE OUT WHO "YOU" ARE IN ORDER TO FIGURE OUT WHAT YOU CAN DO FOR THE COMPETITION...

WHAT'S YOUR FAVORITE COLOR?
BLUE? I DON'T KNOW!

WHAT WORD DESCRIBES YOU BEST?

NOT NORMAL.

OK...THAT'S TWO WORDS. BUT WHAT DO YOU MEAN?
I'M THE ONLY ONE IN CLASS WHO HAS TO GO TO THE HOSPITAL, EVERYONE THINKS I'M WEIRD, AND I'M PRETTY SURE MY BRAIN IS BROKEN.

YOUR BRAIN ISN'T BROKEN, YOU JUST SAY THINGS WITHOUT THINKING SOMETIMES.
YEAH, BUT THAT'S JUST ONE THING. THERE ARE LOADS OF OTHER THINGS.
I JUST FEEL LIKE I'M FROM A DIFFERENT UNIVERSE...
I THINK MY MAM'S FROM A DIFFERENT UNIVERSE, TOO.

ANYWAY, ARE YOU LOOKING FORWARD TO THE FIELD TRIP?
YEAH! MS. JONES ALWAYS PICKS THE BEST PLACES.

I CAN'T BELIEVE THIS WILL BE OUR LAST FIELD TRIP.
WELL, YOU NEVER KNOW! THEY MIGHT HAVE FIELD TRIPS NEXT YEAR?

YEAH, MAYBE THEY'LL TAKE US TO SPACE!

THAT WOULD BE SO COOL! I DON'T THINK THEY HAVE WAFFLES THERE, THOUGH.

IS IT TRUE THAT YOU GET MORE HOMEWORK IN HIGH SCHOOL?

YEAH! I'M ACTUALLY REALLY LOOKING FORWARD TO IT! THEY SAY IT TAKES, ON AVERAGE, SIX HOURS TO COMPLETE EVERY NIGHT.

OH NO!
UGH!
NOT AGAIN!
FRESH GUM

ARE WE CURSED? I THINK WE'RE CURSED.
THIS IS BEYOND BAD LUCK.

AT THIS STAGE, I WOULDN'T BE SURPRISED.

WHERE ARE
MY SWEETS?
GIMME THEM!

KNOCK KNOCK

IT'S YOUR MAM!
AWWWW! BUT SHE WASN'T SUPPOSED TO PICK ME UP UNTIL SEVEN.

SAM'S MAM IS NICE. SHE SELLS STUFF DOOR TO DOOR.
RANDOM STUFF NOBODY NEEDS

FED UP WITH RUBBING YOUR DOG? LET HIM PET HIMSELF WITH THE PET PATTER 3000!
DOGS LOVE IT

DON'T WANT TO CLEAN YOUR KITCHEN EVER AGAIN? ROBOMOP HAS YOU COVERED!

THE ELDERLY CAN STILL HAVE FUN, TOO! ELDER SKATES – TAKE YOUR GRANNY TO THE PARK FOR A SPIN!

I BETTER GO, SEE YOU IN SCHOOL!
SEE YA!
THE NEXT DAY
HAPPY SHOPPING
SALE
FRESH
EVERY SUNDAY, WE GO SHOPPING WITH MAM.

BAKERY
AKE
MAM, CAN WE GET ICE CREAM AND SIT AT THE FOUNTAIN?
GREAT IDEA!

THIS IS THE FOUNTAIN. ABBEY FELL IN ONCE, SO SHE'S NOT ALLOWED TO SIT THERE ON HER OWN.
FLORIST
PLAYER

MAM, ABBEY'S TRYING TO MAKE THE CONE STICK TO HER FACE AGAIN!
ABBEY! HOW MANY TIMES DO I HAVE TO TELL YOU NOT TO DO THAT?

THE SMELL OF SHOPPING CENTER TOILETS IS LITERALLY THE WORST.
MAM...

NEARLY DONE!

SUE! HOW ARE YOU? I HAVEN'T SEEN YOU IN YEARS!
OH MY GOD, GINA!

AND WHO IS THIS LITTLE ONE? MY, SHE LOOKS JUST LIKE HER DADDY!
YEAH, SHE ACTS LIKE HIM, TOO! THIS IS ABBEY. ABBEY, SAY HI.

HI!

ABBEY DOES ACT LIKE JERRY. SHE'S ALWAYS MOANING.

HANG ON A SEC. WHAT IF I ACT LIKE MY DAD?! WHAT IF HE'S AN ALIEN...

I CAN'T REMEMBER MY DAD. HE LEFT WHEN I WAS ONLY A BABY.

SOMETIMES I THINK ABOUT HIM AND WONDER WHERE HE IS AND IF HE WONDERS WHERE I AM.

DAD FACTS
HAS GREEN ALIEN EYES
IS FUSSY WITH FOOD, JUST LIKE ME
MAM DOESN'T LIKE TALKING ABOUT HIM. I DON'T KNOW WHY. I ASK HER ABOUT HIM EVERY COUPLE OF MONTHS, THOUGH, AND TAKE DOWN NOTES.

WHAT I THINK MY DAD IS LIKE

MAM, CAN I CALL SAM?

BUT YOU SPENT THE WHOLE DAY TOGETHER YESTERDAY!

HOME
KEEP IT DOWN, OK? JERRY IS ASLEEP.

SAM! WHAT IF MY DAD IS AN ALIEN! ABBEY ACTS JUST LIKE JERRY, SO WHAT IF I ACT LIKE MY DAD?
WHOA! SLOW DOWN!

I NEED TO FIND HIM!
DO YOU EVEN KNOW WHERE HE LIVES? IS HIS NAME ON YOUR BIRTH CERTIFICATE?

NO...AND I DON'T KNOW...AND WHY?
JUST FIND IT AND BRING IT TO SCHOOL.

I KNOW WHERE IT IS, BUT I DON'T THINK I CAN GET IT.
GIANT SPIDER

BUT SOMETIMES WHEN YOU REALLY WANT SOMETHING, YOU HAVE TO BE BRAVE. ON A BRAVE METER, I WEIGH IN AT A SOLID TWO AND A HALF OUT OF TEN.
Zzz

MUST...

BE...

REALLY...

QUIE—

THE KEYS ARE IN THE DISHWASHER, LOVE. NO, I DON'T WANT ANY HAM.

I CAN DO THIS, I CAN DO THIS...

OK. HERE GOES NOTHING...

IT'S A LOT BIGGER UNDER HERE THAN I THOUGHT.

THERE IT IS!

GOT IT!

POOT

WHAT IF THIS IS A BAD IDEA?
WHAT IF I GET IN TROUBLE?
WHAT IF I GET SAM IN TROUBLE?

SOMEONE'S COMING!

NIGHT NIGHT.

THAT WAS CLOSE!

CHAPTER 4

SUPER WEIRDOS UNITE!

THE NEXT MORNING
SPORTS DAY
BAKE SALE
YOU LOOK AWFUL!
THANKS.

BIRTH CERTIFICATE
MARK SAUNDERS...

GREAT! NOW WE HAVE HIS SIGNATURE! SO, THE PLAN IS...

WHAT'S THIS?

NADINE! GIVE IT BACK!
WHAT ARE YOU GONNA DO?
JUMP AND GET IT?

GIVE IT BACK!
NADINE!

OH MY GOD... NICE HAIRSTYLE, REBECCA!

HOPE YOU GOT A REFUND.

SIT DOWN! WHAT'S ALL THIS SCREAMING ABOUT?
SHAUNA, WHERE'S YOUR BOW TIE?
I DON'T KNOW, TEACHER. I COULDN'T FIND IT.

WELL, YOU KNOW WHAT THAT MEANS.

EVERYONE, SIT DOWN! IT'S TIME FOR YOUR TEST.

MATH WEEK
TEST?! I COMPLETELY FORGOT!

I HOPE YOU'VE ALL STUDIED. THIS WILL BE GOING TOWARD YOUR FINAL GRADES...

I CAN'T BELIEVE I FORGOT ABOUT THE TEST!

GOSSIP

I DON'T KNOW THE ANSWER TO THIS QUESTION.
OR THIS ONE!
I'M GOING TO FAIL AND BE GROUNDED FOREVER...

COME ON, BRAIN! CONCENTRATE!

AHHHHHHH!!!

IS HER HEAD SPINNING?

DON'T WORRY, I'M SURE YOU'LL PASS.
YEAH, RIGHT...

YOU LOOK LIKE A BOY!
DOES YOUR HEAD FEEL WEIRD?
CAN I TOUCH IT?
WHAT HAPPENED?

HEY, WANT TO SIT WITH US?

SO, WHERE'S ALL YOUR HAIR GONE...?

MY MAM CUT IT OFF.
WELL...I THINK IT LOOKS COOL!

YOU LOOK LIKE A PUNK!
REBECCA

I WISH WE HAD SUPERPOWERS.
THE SUPER WEIRDOS
R

ONE OF MY POWERS WOULD BE TO DO MY HOMEWORK IN LESS THAN FIVE SECONDS.
FINISHED! NOW TIME TO LISTEN TO MUSIC.

ANOTHER WOULD BE HAVING AN INVISIBILITY WATCH, SO I CAN DISAPPEAR.
STAY OUT FRANKIE!!
HE HE
WHO SAID THAT?!

IT WOULD COME IN HANDY FOR CHORES, TOO...
FRANKIE? HELLO?

SAM'S SUPERPOWER WOULD BE READING MINDS.
YOU'RE THINKING ABOUT CRACKLE DOING A TIKTOK DANCE.

REBECCA'S INHALER WOULD HAVE THE POWER TO FREEZE BULLIES IN REAL TIME, TOO.

THAT'S WHAT I'LL DO FOR THE COMPETITION!

OWW!

I'M GONNA GET YOU ON THE FIELD TRIP, FREAK!

MAM...AM I
A FREAK?
A FREAK?
OF COURSE NOT!
WHY WOULD YOU
SAY THAT?

JUST
WONDERING.

I KNOW HOW UPSET YOU
GET WHEN PEOPLE SAY
HORRIBLE THINGS.
IT'S LIKE YOU AND
SAM ARE THE ONLY ONES
WHO UNDERSTAND ME. WITH
EVERYONE ELSE, IT FEELS LIKE
I'M SPEAKING A DIFFERENT
LANGUAGE.

TONY'S TAKEAWAY
14
14
OPEN
THE TRUTH IS, SOME PEOPLE ARE JUST SO AFRAID TO BE THEMSELVES.

DON'T EVER BE AFRAID TO BE YOURSELF. I LEARNED THAT TOO LATE IN LIFE.
BURGERS
SNACK BOX
DEAL

YOU'RE SMART, FUNNY, AND KIND. DON'T LET ANYONE MAKE YOU FEEL SMALL.
BUT I AM SMALL!
YOU KNOW WHAT I MEAN!

TODAY, SOME OF YOU WILL RECEIVE YOUR YELLOW BELT STRIPES. WE'LL BE SPARRING, TOO!

EVERYONE, GET INTO PAIRS.

YOU KNOW, YOU'VE IMPROVED A LOT OVER THE LAST COUPLE OF WEEKS. YOU SHOULD BE REALLY PROUD OF YOURSELF. I CAN SEE A HUGE DIFFERENCE IN YOU.

OK! FRANKIE ANNNND HMM, LET ME SEE... DEBBIE!

OK. YOU CAN DO THIS! YOU CAN DO THIS!

FREAK

BLOCK

I DON'T KNOW HOW I DID IT, BUT
I GOT MY YELLOW STRIPES!

MAYBE I DO HAVE A SUPERPOWER.
THE SUPERPOWER TO KICK BUTT!

SEE, I TOLD YOU!

MAM!

MAM!

WHERE'S MAM?

WHY
IS ABBEY
HERE?

MAM'S IN THE HOSPITAL.

DON'T WORRY. QUICK, PUT YOUR SEAT BELT ON.

THAT'S THE THING WHEN YOUR MAM'S SICK. YOU ALWAYS WORRY SOMETHING LIKE THIS IS GOING TO HAPPEN.

ICU

ICU
X RAY

SHE WAS HAVING PALPITATIONS. SHE'S STABLE NOW BUT NEEDS TO REST.

CHAPTER 5

NANA AND GRANDAD'S HOUSE

LATER
DLES
PUNK
IS MAM GOING TO BE OK?
I HAVE TO GET BACK TO THE HOSPITAL BUT I'LL TAKE YOU TO NANA AND GRANDAD'S FIRST.

ARE YOU GETTING YOUR THINGS READY, ABBEY?
FRANKIE!!
YEAH!

HOW AM I SUPPOSED TO FOCUS ON ANYTHING? I DON'T KNOW WHAT'S GOING ON AND NO ONE IS TALKING ABOUT IT.

I LIKE STAYING AT MY NANA AND GRANDAD'S. THEY HAVE LOADS OF OLD PICTURES EVERYWHERE. SOME ARE REALLY FUNNY, TOO!

NANA MAKES THE BEST DINNERS!

AND DESSERTS!
GIANT BOWL OF ICE CREAM

THEY ONLY HAVE TWO BEDROOMS, THOUGH, SO YOU KNOW WHAT THAT MEANS...
ROOMIES!

THREE REASONS NOT TO SHARE A ROOM WITH ABBEY...
SHE DOESN'T UNDERSTAND THE WORD PRIVACY
WHOA! ARE THESE NANA'S?
SHE FARTS IN HER SLEEP
SHE SOUNDS LIKE A SEAGULL WHEN SHE SINGS

FRANKIE! LOOK!
STOP! I'M TRYING TO DRAW...

WHOA!

AHHHH!!!

NOOOOO!!!

WHAT'S HAPPENED, PET?
FRANKIE, IT WAS AN ACCIDENT!
YEAH RIGHT! YOU DID IT ON PURPOSE.

YOU KNOW, I DIDN'T HAVE A SISTER GROWING UP. I HAD FOUR BROTHERS!

YOU TWO NEED TO STICK TOGETHER! YOU'RE LUCKY TO HAVE EACH OTHER.

GET WELL

SOON

TO MAM

HOPE YOU GET BETTER SOON, AND COME HOME ~~SOON~~ THIS WEEK. WE MISS YOU

THE NEXT DAY
COME ON, IRELAND!
COME ON!
BASKETBALL IS BORING...

NANA AND GRANDAD LOVE BASKETBALL. THAT'S MY AUNTY ON THE TV. SHE'S A COACH.
THAT WAS A STINKIN' FOUL!

FRANKIE, YOU COULD BE THE NEXT PLAYER IN OUR FAMILY!

SHE REALLY HASN'T SEEN ME ON SPORTS DAY...
YEAH! HA HA.

GOOD EFFORT MEDAL

NO, SHE'S GONNA BE AN ARTIST! ISN'T THAT RIGHT?
YEP! LOOK AT MY PICTURE FOR THE ART COMPETITION.

THAT'S BRILLIANT! GOOD LUCK, CHAMP!

EVEN THOUGH I HAD FIGURED OUT WHAT TO DO FOR THE COMPETITION, I STILL WANTED TO FIND MY DAD.

SAM HAS AN AMAZING PLAN...
I MADE A FAKE PETITION SO WE CAN PRETEND WE'RE COLLECTING SIGNATURES.
WHEN HE SIGNS IT, WE CAN MATCH IT TO THE BIRTH CERTIFICATE.

THERE ARE ONLY TWO HOUSES REGISTERED TO A MARK SAUNDERS, SO IT HAS TO BE ONE OF THESE.

WHEN WILL WE GO?
AFTER THE FIELD TRIP, WHEN THE BUS DROPS US BACK AT THE SCHOOL.

BE KIND
ROOM 12
IS YOUR MAM OK?
I DON'T KNOW, I'M GOING TO SEE HER LATER ON.
NO ONE'S REALLY TALKING ABOUT IT. NOT TO ME, ANYWAY.
I HOPE SHE'S HOME SOON, THOUGH. I DON'T THINK I CAN SHARE A ROOM WITH ABBEY FOR MUCH LONGER.
HEY!

KNOCK, KNOCK!
NO ONE'S HOME.

I HAVE ENOUGH ON MY PLATE WITHOUT HAVING TO DEAL WITH NADINE, TOO.

DON'T FORGET ABOUT THE FIELD TRIP!

ART CLASS – COMPETITION TIME!
I KNOW YOU'VE ALL BEEN WORKING HARD OVER THE LAST WEEK!
NOW, THE PICTURE WITH THE MOST VOTES BY THE CLASS WILL BE THE WINNER.

I THINK IT'S GOOD? I HOPE IT'S GOOD, I...

YOU'VE GOT MY VOTE!
SAM, YOU LOOK LIKE WONDER WOMAN!
LOOK AT THE COLORS!
THAT'S SO COOL!

HOW COME SHE WON?! IT'S NOT EVEN THAT GOOD.

THIS ISN'T FAIR!

IT'S BETTER THAN YOURS, IN FAIRNESS.

BEAUTY
·KIND
·LOVELY
·ACTUAL MODEL

I CAN'T BELIEVE I ACTUALLY WON!
MY ART ON OUR CLASSROOM DOOR!
ROOM 14
1ST
ART
CLASS

WOO-HOO!
WE'LL HAVE TO CELEBRATE LATER. WAIT UNTIL YOUR MAM HEARS THIS!

MAM!
FRANKIE! ABBEY!

I WON THE ART COMPETITION IN SCHOOL TODAY!

WOW! YELLOW STRIPES AND NOW AN ART COMPETITION? I CAN'T KEEP UP WITH YOU!
I KNOW!

AND WE MADE YOU THIS.
I LOVE IT!

I DON'T LIKE SEEING MY MAM IN THE HOSPITAL. ESPECIALLY WHEN SHE HAS WIRES AND TUBES EVERYWHERE.

SORRY. VISITATION TIME IS NEARLY OVER.
106

BUT WE ONLY JUST GOT HERE!

I GAVE NANA MONEY FOR YOUR FIELD TRIP. HAVE A GREAT TIME!
LOVE YOU, MAM.
AND DON'T WORRY. I'LL BE HOME SOON, SWEETHEART.

LATER
HELLO? ANYONE THERE? FRANKIE WHO? HOLD ON ONE SECOND.

OH SORRY, PET. MY HEARING AIDS ARE OFF AGAIN! IT'S SAM.
NANA, I'M RIGHT HERE!

HEY, WHAT'S UP?
SO...I CAN'T GO ON THE FIELD TRIP TOMORROW.

WHAT? WHY NOT?

MY MAM'S COUSIN ROGER DIED.
I'M REALLY SORRY, SAM.

OH NO! WHAT ABOUT THE PLAN TO FIND MY DAD? YOU HAVE TO COME ON THE FIELD TRIP!
I'LL ASK AGAIN WHEN MY MAM STOPS CRYING, BUT IT MIGHT BE A WHILE...

IT WAS SOME KIND OF FOOD-EATING CONTEST. APPARENTLY HE ATE TOO MANY CHICKEN WINGS.

THAT CAN HAPPEN?
ANYWAY, HIS WAKE IS TOMORROW MORNING.

I HAVE TO HELP SAM. SHE CAN'T MISS THE FIELD TRIP!
HMM, I WONDER IF A DISGUISE WILL WORK.

REBECCA
08563
I'LL DEFINITELY NEED BACKUP.

THE NEXT DAY
EVERYONE IS GOING TO SEE US!
HERE, TRY THESE ON.

PERFECT!

THEY SAID HE ATE ABOUT TWENTY BOWLS OF WINGS.
OK, GO!

6
I LOOK RIDICULOUS.
IT'S CALLED ACTING, JUST GO WITH IT!

CHAPTER 6

HEY!
IS SAM...

UM, I MEAN,
ROGER. WE'RE
OLD FRIENDS.

ROGER
I CAN'T BELIEVE THAT ACTUALLY WORKED.

EWW, WHY DO THEY JUST LEAVE YOU LYING OUT LIKE THAT?
I DON'T KNOW. IN CASE ANYONE WANTS ONE LAST SELFIE?

I'VE NEVER SEEN SOMEONE CRY WHILE EATING A SANDWICH BEFORE.
THE LAST THING I'D WANT IN MY COFFIN IS SOMEONE ELSE'S CRUMBS.

SAM'S MAM!

THIS ISN'T GOING TO WORK! WE'RE GONNA GET CAUGHT!
RELAX, SHE DOESN'T EVEN KNOW WE'RE HERE.

WHAT ON EARTH ARE YOU GIRLS DOING HERE?

EHH, WE CAME TO SAY GOODBYE TO OUR GOOD FRIEND ROG—
IT'S ME, YOU HAM! WHAT ARE YOU DOING HERE?

Roger
WOULD ANYONE LIKE TO SAY A FEW WORDS?

QUICK! WE'RE SNEAKING YOU OUT SO YOU CAN COME ON THE FIELD TRIP!
COME ON, LET'S GO!
PUT THIS OVER YOUR HEAD!

SAM! HOW ARE YOU, LOVEY? I HEAR YOU'RE DOING GREAT IN SCHOOL!
YEAH, SCHOOL... IT'S GOOD...

WELL, WHEN MY GREGORY LEFT ELEMENTARY SCHOOL, HE...
THAT'S GREAT, AUNT MAY, BUT I HAVE TO GO STUDY. I'VE GOT A TEST TOMORROW!

OH!

YOU KNOW, MY GREGORY...

ROGER WAS A GOOD MAN. HE LOVED COLLECTING THESE TINY FIGURINES.
Roger
HE HAD WELL OVER TWO HUNDRED OF THE CUTE LITTLE FELLAS AT ONE STAGE.

THIS ONE'S NAME IS CLAUDINE.

WHAT'S THAT NOISE?

IT SOUNDS LIKE A HIGH-PITCHED SCREAM RIPPING THROUGH MY EARS.

COME ON!

IT'S A GHOST!
ARGH! BANSHEE! BANSHEE!!

THERE'S ALWAYS SOMETHING...
AHHHH!

HURRY!
QUICK, WE'VE ONLY GOT FIFTEEN MINUTES TO GET TO SCHOOL.

I THINK THAT WAS THE FASTEST I'VE EVER RUN IN MY LIFE.
WATER!

I'M GLAD MS. JONES ORGANIZED THIS YEAR'S FIELD TRIP.
HI, GIRLS!

LAST YEAR'S WAS A DISASTER!
MATH MUSEUM

OK, EVERYONE! WE'LL BE GOING SWIMMING FIRST AND THEN TO THE BOG.
I HOPE YOU ALL REMEMBERED A SPARE PAIR OF CLOTHES! THE BOG IS VERY MUCKY.

ALL I CAN THINK OF IS NADINE GETTING ME ON THE FIELD TRIP.

WHAT IF SHE TRIES TO GET ME AT THE SWIMMING POOL?
WOULD YOU RATHERRRRR, EAT BRAINS FOR BREAKFAST EVERY MORNING OR HAVE FISH FOR FEET?

ALL RIGHT, WHO NEEDS TO USE THE BATHROOM? HURRY UP.
FOLLOW ME ON TIK TOK

WOULD YOU RATHER...

I KNOW REBECCA WAS ONLY TRYING TO CHEER ME UP, BUT IT WAS HARD TO FOCUS ON ANYTHING OTHER THAN NADINE'S BANANA FISTS.

I DON'T GET WHY SHE HATES ME SO MUCH. I'VE NEVER ACTUALLY DONE ANYTHING TO HER.

I JUST WISH I COULD SAY SOMETHING. BUT EVERY TIME I TRY TO, I CAN'T!
YOU GONNA SAY SOMETHING??
UMM...

WE FINALLY ARRIVED. THE POOL WAS GIGANTIC! WE WERE HAVING SO MUCH FUN THAT I ALMOST FORGOT HOW WORRIED I WAS.
NO DIVING
HEY, LOOK AT ME! I'M A WALRUS!

ARE YOU NERVOUS FOR LATER?
YEAH. I'M WORRIED HE WON'T BE NICE. WHAT IF HE'S MEAN LIKE NADINE?

DON'T BE THINKING LIKE THAT. HE'S JUST AS LIKELY TO BE NICE. YOU WON'T KNOW UNTIL YOU MEET HIM.

I'M STARVING!
SAME! I'M GOING TO GET A MILKSHAKE!
I'M GETTING CURLY FRIES.

WHAT IS THAT? WHY DO YOU HAVE A BANDAGE ON YOUR BUTT?
NO WAY!

YOU HAVE HOLES IN YOUR UNDERWEAR! ARE YOU POOR?
I THOUGHT YOU WERE A FREAK BEFORE, BUT THIS JUST TOPS THE CHARTS!

HA HA HA HA HA
GO AWAY! GO AWAY! GO AWAY!

I COULDN'T TELL MS. JONES BECAUSE I DIDN'T WANT THE WHOLE CLASS TO KNOW I HAVE A BIG STUPID BANDAGE ON MY BUTT.
YOU GIRLS READY? WE'RE LEAVING SOON!
SHE'S THE REAL FREAK, NOT YOU!

THAT WAS THE MOST EMBARRASSING THING THAT'S EVER HAPPENED TO ME.

LATER AT THE BOG
OK, EVERYONE, GET INTO TEAMS OF TWO!

SAM, WE'LL TAKE THE TRAIL.
GREAT...
TRAIL

A NATURE TRAIL WITH CRACKLE IS MY WORST NIGHTMARE.
LOOK! AN ACORN!
I HATE ACORNS!
PLONK

GETTING TO JUMP IN MUD IS ACTUALLY SO MUCH FUN.
CANNONBALL!

HEY, WHY ARE YOU SO NICE TO ME?
I DON'T KNOW. BECAUSE YOU'RE MY FRIEND?

I'VE NEVER HAD A FRIEND BEFORE.

HEY LOOK, IT'S THE TWO FOREST FREAKS.
GOOD ONE!

GET HER!
BOOM! HA HA! YEAH!

FRANKIE!

YOU DIDN'T EVEN DESERVE TO WIN THE ART COMPETITION!
YOU ONLY WON BECAUSE YOUR MAM IS IN THE HOSPITAL.

HEY, WHEEZY.
HA HA!

WHAT THE...
YOU WEREN'T
SUPPOSED TO
GET BACK UP!

BLOCK
SHAUNA!
GET HER!

I GUESS KARATE LESSONS
REALLY CAME IN HANDY!
SLAP

I'M GLAD I DIDN'T WEAR MY GOOD CLOTHES ON THE FIELD TRIP.
NADINE! I DIDN'T MEAN TO!

WHAT'S THAT SMELL?

THE FIELD TRIP WASN'T THAT BAD, I SUPPOSE.
I'M BASICALLY A NINJA NOW.
DID YOU SEE HER FACE WHEN YOU STOOD UP?! IT WAS AWESOME.
I CAN'T BELIEVE I MISSED THIS!

HOLD STILL!
I AM!

ANYWAY, YOU READY?
I'M READY!
I BROUGHT SOME BRAIN LICKERS FOR THE ROAD!

WHEN MAM TOLD ME THAT DAD MOVED AWAY WHEN I WAS A BABY, DID SHE MEAN TO SPACE? IT WOULD EXPLAIN WHY I HAVEN'T SEEN HIM.
30
PHARM
DO YOU THINK MY DAD LIKES ICE CREAM?
I DON'T KNOW IF ALIENS LIKE COLD FOOD.
OOH! CAN WE GET SOME ICE CREAM? I'M HUNGRY AGAIN!

CHAPTER 7

BEING NORMAL IS BORING

WHAT'S THAT?
IT'S A FANTA FLOAT! WANNA TRY?
FLORIST

IT LOOKS GROSS.

NO, I'M GOOD, THANKS.
THE ONE WITH COKE IS BETTER ANYWAY.

I CAN'T BELIEVE YOU'RE GOING TO MEET YOUR DAD! I'D BE SO NERVOUS!

I DON'T KNOW HOW I FEEL, BUT MY BRAIN HASN'T STOPPED THINKING ALL DAY.
ALERT
I CAN'T FIND HOW SHE'S FEELING!
SAVE YOURSELVES!
I CAN'T THINK STRAIGHT WITH ALL THIS NOISE!

WHO LEFT A BRAIN LICKER IN THE FEELINGS DRAWER?

FRANKIE?
SORRY, I ZONED OUT!

MEALS
WE NEED TO THINK OF SOME QUESTIONS TO ASK.

THE FIRST WILL BE "WHAT MUSIC DO YOU LIKE?"

WHAT ABOUT "WHAT'S YOUR FAVORITE FOOD?"
THAT'S A GOOD ONE! AND "DO YOU LIKE IT WHEN YOUR FOOD TOUCHES?" I HATE THAT!

YOU COULD ASK WHAT HE WAS LIKE AT YOUR AGE?
I WONDER IF HE HATES BAD SMELLS, TOO?
ONCE, MY MAM FARTED GOING THROUGH A CAR WASH AND IT WAS SO BAD, I WAS SICK IN MY PENCIL CASE.

SO, HOW ARE YOU GOING TO INTRODUCE YOURSELF?

HEY, I'M FRANKIE, AND YOU'RE MY DAD!

OK, BUT I THINK WE NEED TO STICK TO THE PLAN, JUST IN CASE!

SALE

IS THIS PART OF THE PLAN?
WE NEED THIS!
SUPER MARIO YOSHI'S ISLAND!

DO YOU KNOW HOW HARD IT IS TO GET THIS? AND LOOK AT THE PRICE!
I'VE NEVER PLAYED MARIO...

YOU CAN PLAY WITH US, BUT JUST DON'T SAY THAT TO ANYONE EVER AGAIN.

I WONDER IF ALIENS PLAY VIDEO GAMES. WHAT IF THEY INVENTED THEM?

FASHION
CHERS

I THINK YOU NEED A MAKEOVER.

HERE, TRY THIS!

ARE YOU JOKING?

NOW THAT'S WHAT I'M TALKING ABOUT!
HOW ABOUT THIS?

LET US SEE!

OK! I'M READY!

ONLY MESSING!

NOW ALL YOU NEED IS SOME PERFUME SO YOU DON'T SMELL LIKE A BOG!

WHAT DOES YOUR HAIR LOOK LIKE DOWN?

YEAH, I THINK IT LOOKS BETTER UP, ACTUALLY...

NIGHT Wear
LOOK! IT'S CRACKLE IN THE WILD!
AND SHE'S LOOKING AT UNDERWEAR!

LET ME SEE!
SHE'S COMING!

HE HE
SHH

LET'S GO!

I THINK THIS IS NEAR MY NANA AND GRANDAD'S HOUSE!
IT'S ON THIS ROAD SOMEWHERE...

BEWARE
OF DOG

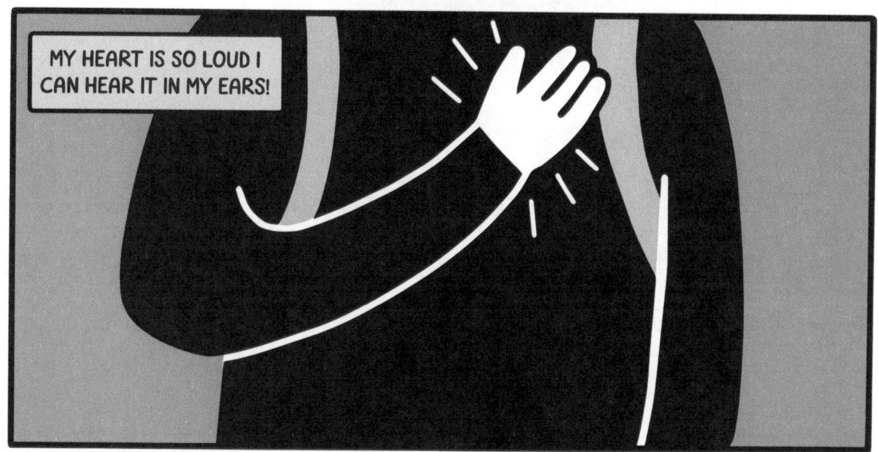
MY HEART IS SO LOUD I CAN HEAR IT IN MY EARS!

JUST BREATHE...

UGGGH!

YEP, THAT'S
A FRESH ONE!

IT'S OK, IT'S
COMING OFF.

HEY,
YOU!

YOU BETTER
NOT BE STANDING
ON MY ROSES!

8

GO!

THIS IS IT, THE FIRST HOUSE! NUMBER 68.

SAY HELLO TO ALL YOUR BROTHERS AND SISTERS...

MEANWHILE, IN MY BRAIN...

I FEEL SICK.

KNOCK
KNOCK

TRY AGAIN! MAYBE THEY DIDN'T HEAR.

REMEMBER THE PLAN! JUST ASK IF THEY'D LIKE TO SIGN OUR PETITION.

I HEARD YOU THE FIRST TIME!

MAYBE WE SHOULD JUST GO?

WELL, WHO IS IT?

HI, WOULD YOU LIKE TO SIGN OUR PETITION?

SORRY FOR TALKING THROUGH THE MAIL BOX.
68
I ONLY OPEN THE DOOR WHEN I'M EXPECTING SOMEONE. COME IN!

SO, WHAT'S THE PETITION FOR?

IT'S TO START A SCIENCE CLUB! BECAUSE SCIENCE IS SO GREAT...
DO YOU GIRLS THINK I WAS BORN YESTERDAY?

I'M LOOKING FOR MY DAD. WE THINK HE LIVES HERE. HIS NAME IS MARK SAUNDERS?

MY HUSBAND'S NAME WAS MARK, BUT HE WAS OLD ENOUGH TO BE YOUR GRANDAD! HE WAS 68!

WHY ARE YOU TRYING TO FIND HIM?
BECAUSE EVERYONE THINKS I'M DIFFERENT...AND I FEEL DIFFERENT AND I DON'T KNOW WHY.

HONEY, THERE'S NOTHING WRONG WITH BEING DIFFERENT.
IN FACT, IT'S THE BEST THING YOU CAN BE!

I'D HATE TO BE NORMAL.
IT'S BORING! LOOK, THIS IS
ME IN THE 1980S.
AUG 1984
WOW!
THAT'S YOU?
YOU'RE A PUNK!

YEP! STILL AM.
PEOPLE THINK ONCE YOU'RE
OLD, YOU HAVE TO GO OUT
ON ELDER SKATES.

CHAPTER 8

GRADUATION

I CAN'T TELL NANA AND GRANDAD WHERE I REALLY WAS AFTER THE FIELD TRIP.
WHERE HAVE YOU BEEN? THE FIELD TRIP FINISHED AT THREE O'CLOCK!
WE WERE WORRIED SICK! DO YOU KNOW WHAT TIME IT IS?
BUSTED!

I TOLD THEM I GOT LOST AND NANA CALLED JERRY, AND NOW I'M GROUNDED FOR A WHOLE MONTH!

HOW AM I GOING TO FIND MY DAD NOW?!
ABBEY, PUT *WHEEL OF FORTUNE* ON!

THE NEXT DAY
WHAT HAPPENED TO YOU?
GOT MY PHONE TAKEN FROM ME, GROUNDED FOR THREE WEEKS. SHE SAID I GOT OFF LIGHTLY AFTER THE WHOLE ROGER THING.

I DIDN'T GET GROUNDED, BUT I HAVE DOUBLE THE CHORES.
I'M GROUNDED FOR A MONTH!

THIS IS SO ANNOYING. WE SHOULD BE HAPPY! THIS IS OUR LAST WEEK IN SCHOOL!
FRANKIE! SIT DOWN.

SCHOOL WAS RUBBISH TODAY. AND WHEN I GOT HOME, THINGS DIDN'T GET MUCH BETTER.
YOU CAN FINISH YOUR HOMEWORK AND GET READY FOR BED!
BUT IT'S ONLY EIGHT O'CLOCK!
CAN I WATCH CARTOONS?

KNOCK

SURPRISE!
MAM!

I MISSED YOU SO MUCH!
I MISSED YOU WAY MORE THAN FRANKIE.

OK, OK! THAT'S ENOUGH HUGS FOR NOW!

THANKS FOR MINDING THEM, MAM.
NOT AT ALL! WE LOVE HAVING THEM STAY.

AND I HEARD WHAT YOU DID, TOO. WE'LL TALK ABOUT IT AT HOME.

DOUBLE BUSTED.

BACK TO MY FAVORITE PLACE.
HOSPITAL

MAM IS STILL MAD AT ME...

AHEM!

I'M SORRY,
MAM.

YOU JUST CAN'T BE RUNNING OFF LIKE THAT, FRANKIE.

I KNOW.

W X
Y
FRANKIE!
HOW ARE YOU? YOU
MUST BE EXCITED FOR
THE SUMMER?
PLEASE GIVE US
SOME GOOD NEWS TODAY,
DOCTOR. I NEED IT.

YOUR MAM MUST BE A
PSYCHIC BECAUSE IT'S BRILLIANT NEWS,
ACTUALLY! YOU DON'T HAVE TO COME TO
APPOINTMENTS ANYMORE, AS YOU'VE
GROWN SO MUCH!
REALLY?!
YES, AND
YOU CAN STOP
GETTING INJECTIONS
NOW, TOO.

WELL, THAT'S ONE WAY TO START THE SUMMER!
YEAH, IF I WASN'T GROUNDED...

FINALLY! THE LAST DAY OF SCHOOL.
I'D LIKE TO START BY SAYING WELL DONE TO EVERYONE FOR COMPLETING THE YEAR.

I CAN'T BELIEVE WE'RE FINALLY FINISHED.
NO MORE CRACKLE!
NO MORE HAUNTED BOW TIES!

FUN
PICASSO

WILL YOU SIGN MY SHIRT?
WILL YOU SIGN MINE?

I DON'T NEED LOADS OF SIGNATURES BECAUSE I HAVE THE BEST TWO IN CLASS.
SAM
REBECCA

THERE WAS ONE LAST THING I REALLY WASN'T LOOKING FORWARD TO...
FRANKIE, YOUR MATH RESULTS!

C+

NO WAY! I CAN'T BELIEVE IT!
I GOT AN A!

I DIDN'T FAIL MATH!
SAM

NATURE
A
SAM
AND ART WAS EVEN BETTER, I GOT MY FIRST A. MAYBE MY BRAIN DOES WORK!

IT DOESN'T LOOK LIKE NADINE GOT GOOD NEWS, THOUGH.
6TH GRADE
SHUT UP!

6TH GRADE GRADUATION

SO, YOU GOING TO MISS THIS PLACE?
I'M GOING TO MISS IT LIKE I MISS WATCHING GOLF... WHICH IS NOT AT ALL!

I'LL MISS ART CLASS, BUT THAT'S ABOUT IT!
ME TOO! MS. JONES IS THE BEST!

AFTER SCHOOL, I COULDN'T WAIT TO TELL SENSEI THAT I STOOD UP FOR MYSELF.
AND THEN SHE WENT TO PUNCH ME AND I BLOCKED LIKE THIS!

I WAS JUST LIKE YOU ONCE, YOU KNOW.

BRIAN WATTS WAS HIS NAME. HE MADE MY LIFE HARD.

HOW DID YOU GET HIM TO STOP?
IT WENT ON FOR YEARS. UNTIL I FINALLY LEARNED HOW TO PROTECT MYSELF.

THEN ONE DAY...

BLOCK
WHOA

AFTER THAT, HE NEVER LOOKED AT ME AGAIN!

YOU NEED TO REMEMBER THAT THE PROBLEM ISN'T YOU. OFTEN BULLIES ARE UNHAPPY THEMSELVES.

MAYBE HE WAS RIGHT.

I GOT A GOLD STAR ON MY SPELLING TEST!
WELL DONE, ABBEY! THAT'S BRILLIANT.

I DON'T KNOW WHY I STILL SUPPORT THIS TEAM! THEY'RE USELESS.

I DON'T KNOW HOW I'M GOING TO FIND MY DAD NOW THAT I'M BASICALLY GROUNDED FOREVER.

KNOCK
KNOCK

WHAT ARE YOU GUYS DOING HERE?!
OUR MAMS TALKED AND SAID WE COULD HAVE A SLEEPOVER!

THE LAST COUPLE OF WEEKS HAVE BEEN REALLY HARD, SO I THOUGHT WE COULD CELEBRATE!

SO, WHAT DO YOU THINK OF MARIO KART?
COME ON! GET IT!!!

GAME

YESTERDAY WAS REALLY FUN.
YEAH, IT WAS. IT WOULD HAVE BEEN EVEN MORE FUN IF I DIDN'T GET GROUNDED.
ARE YOU GROUNDED? WE'RE HAVING A SLEEPOVER...

I THINK IT'S PROBABLY JUST FOR TONIGHT AND BACK TO BEING GROUNDED TOMORROW.

OR MAYBE NOT!

YEAH, MAYBE YOU'RE NOT GROUNDED ANYMORE.

I KNOW THIS IS A BAD IDEA, BUT...

SHOULD WE GO TO TOWN TOMORROW, TO THE OTHER HOUSE?

I'M IN!
I DON'T KNOW, I'M NOT SURE HOW MANY MORE CHORES I CAN HANDLE!

OK OK, NO NEED TO PEER PRESSURE!

WE LEAVE AT DAWN!
IS THAT A LINE FROM A MOVIE? BECAUSE IT SOUNDS LIKE IT IS.
CAN YOU JUST LET ME HAVE MY MOMENT!

CHAPTER 9

DAD'S HOUSE

THE NEXT MORNING
YOU ASK, SHE'S YOUR MAM!
NO, YOU ASK!

MAM, CAN WE GO TO THE SHOPPING CENTER TODAY?
SURE, I CAN GIVE YOU A LIFT IN TWENTY MINUTES?

I'M SO NERVOUS, MY STOMACH FEELS LIKE IT'S DOING BACKFLIPS.

LAST SUMMER BEFORE SEVENTH GRADE, GIRLS!
I WONDER IF YOU'LL ALL BE IN THE SAME CLASS AGAIN.
I HOPE SO!

I FEEL BAD LYING TO MAM, BUT THERE WAS NO WAY SHE'D UNDERSTAND.

I'LL PICK YOU UP AT SEVEN! IF YOU NEED ME, JUST USE SAM'S PHONE.
HAVE FUN!

HERE'S THE BUS!

BUS

SUMMER SALE NOW ON

THE RAMP'S BROKEN. YOU'LL HAVE TO WAIT FOR THE NEXT BUS.
€

BUS
BUT...
WELL, THAT WAS RUDE!
SUMMER SALE

THE NEXT BUS TOOK FOREVER TO ARRIVE.
PEW
PEW
I'M NEARLY AT LEVEL THREE NOW!
SO CLOSE!

WILL YOU LOT EVER SHUT UP!

DON'T KNOW WHAT HER PROBLEM IS. THAT NOISE IS WAYYYY MORE ANNOYING...
SERIOUSLY!
CLINK
COLA
CLANK
CLONK

I TOLD YOU NO, CHLOE.
YOU ONLY GOT ONE LAST WEEK!
DO YOU THINK PHONES GROW
ON TREES, DO YOU?
WE WEREN'T EVEN THE LOUDEST.

WHAT ARE
YOU LOOKING AT?
WEIRDO!

I THINK THIS IS OUR STOP COMING UP.

IF MY MAM FINDS OUT WHERE I AM, I'LL BE IN SO MUCH TROUBLE.
WE'LL BE BACK ON TIME, DON'T WORRY. I HAVE A TIMER ON MY PHONE.

NOW ALL WE NEED TO DO IS FIND CAMDEN STREET.
OPEN
• BEV'S BAKERY •
YUM
12
14
VIN
COFFEE
STRAWBERRIES. TWO PACKS FOR THREE EUROS.

HAIR
SALON
FISH

FI
CAN WE
GO, PLEASE?

PLEASE DON'T GET SICK,
PLEASE DON'T GET SICK!

I NEED TO GET A PEG FOR MY NOSE. I CAN STILL SMELL IT!

FRANKIE...

MY PHONE JUST DIED.
WHY DID YOU PLAY THAT STUPID GAME!?
IT'S OK, I HAVE MINE! WHAT'S THE ADDRESS?

THE ADDRESS IS ON MY PHONE. ALL I REMEMBER IS IT'S NUMBER 28 AND JUST OFF CAMDEN STREET!

WELL, THAT NARROWS IT DOWN! WHAT ARE WE GOING TO DO NOW?
SORRY TO RUIN YOUR DAY. YOU COULD JUST, YOU KNOW, GET YOUR OWN PHONE AND KEEP UP WITH THE 21ST CENTURY?

live Music
TOWN 2
TAKEAWAY
OPEN
FOOD →
SUB-
H
STOP FIGHTING! EVERYONE ELSE SEEMS TO BE GOING THIS WAY...

TATTO
HOTEL
OPEN
I THINK WE SHOULD GO THIS...

SAM?! REBECCA??!

HOW CAN I THINK WHEN ALL I CAN HEAR ARE OTHER PEOPLE'S CONVERSATIONS!

RESET!
RESET!

SAM!

HA HA

FRANKIE! OVER HERE!

THAT WAS THE SCARIEST FIVE MINUTES EVER.
LET'S JUST ASK FOR DIRECTIONS IN HERE.
POLICE
YEAH

LOOK, WE'RE HERE, PLEASANT STREET!
THERE'S WILSON AVENUE! IS THAT THE ONE?

ARE YOU GIRLS OK?
YEAH. WE'RE TRYING TO FIGURE OUT HOW TO GET TO WILSON AVENUE.

YOU'LL TAKE A LEFT AS YOU LEAVE, FOLLOW THE ROAD ALL THE WAY UP TO TESCO, TAKE A RIGHT AND A LEFT AND RIGHT AGAIN, PASS THE FLATS, AND YOU'RE THERE!
I FORGOT WHAT YOU SAID AFTER TESCO... COULD YOU SAY THAT AGAIN?

-NICE ONES-
MY HEART FEELS LIKE IT'S GOING TO EXPLODE.

UNCLE DAN'S
NEWSAGENTS
I'VE NEVER BEEN THIS NERVOUS!

IT WASN'T A BIG HOUSE, AND THE PAINT ON THE DOOR WAS FLAKY.
28

OK, I'M GOING TO TAKE SOME DEEP BREATHS AND THEN...
KNOCK KNOCK
26
28

WHAT DID YOU DO THAT FOR? I'M NOT READY!

CAN YOU SIGN
OUR PETITION?

SURE! DO YOU
HAVE A PEN?

IT'S HIM, IT'S MY DAD! IT HAS TO BE!
WE LOOK EXACTLY THE SAME.

I THINK YOU'RE MY DAD!
28

NOW THAT I'M HERE, I DON'T KNOW WHAT TO SAY.

DO I ASK WHY HIM AND MAM BROKE UP?
OR ASK IF HE'S AN ALIEN?
NO, THAT CAN'T BE THE FIRST QUESTION I ASK...

COME ON, BRAIN!
THINK OF QUESTIONS!

I CAN'T BELIEVE IT'S YOU!

HOW DID YOU FIND ME? I ONLY RECENTLY MOVED BACK FROM LONDON.

IF IT WASN'T FOR HER, I PROBABLY WOULDN'T HAVE.
I JUST GOT AN A IN COMPUTERS. I'M KINDA A BIG DEAL.

WHAT KIND OF MUSIC DO YOU LIKE?
ROCK, PUNK, CLASSIC. ALL THE GREATS! I PLAY GUITAR, TOO!

I WAS AFRAID YOU WOULD LIKE POP MUSIC!

HE MADE US TEA AND COOKIES.
MY FAVORITE!

ARE YOU AN ALIEN?

PEOPLE THINK I'M WEIRD. I WANT TO KNOW WHY.
I THOUGHT YOU MIGHT BE WEIRD, TOO.
? ?

I FIND IT HARD TO MAKE FRIENDS. WELL, I HAVE FRIENDS NOW BUT YOU KNOW WHAT I MEAN.
I DO. I REMEMBER WHAT SCHOOL WAS LIKE. I GOT BULLIED PRETTY BADLY.

ME TOO! I STOOD UP TO MY BULLIES THE OTHER DAY!
NO WAY!

WE'RE LIKE THE SAME PERSON.
WHAT'S YOUR FAVORITE FOOD?
WAFFLES.
I LOVE WAFFLES!!

DOES YOUR MAM KNOW YOU'RE HERE? I THINK WE SHOULD CALL HER TO LET HER KNOW YOU'RE ALL OK.
SHE THINKS WE'RE AT THE SHOPPING CENTER.

PLEASE DON'T CALL MY MAM! SHE'LL MAKE ME SELL DOORBELL CHIMES FOR THE REST OF THE SUMMER.

CHAPTER 10

THE ULTIMATE GUIDE TO FRANKIE'S WORLD

WE'RE DOOMED!
DOOMED!
YEAH, I'LL SEE YOU IN 2076, IF YOU'RE STILL ALIVE WHEN I'M NOT GROUNDED.

MY DAD WAS PACING AROUND THE KITCHEN AFTER CALLING MY MAM.

WHEN MAM ARRIVED, SHE DIDN'T GIVE ME A FUNNY LOOK, SHE GAVE ME A DISAPPOINTED ONE.
(TRUST ME, I KNOW WHAT IT LOOKS LIKE)
ON A LEVEL BETWEEN 0 TO DISAPPOINTED THIS IS DISAPPOINTED X 10

WE'RE JUST GOING TO HAVE A QUICK CHAT. WE WON'T BE LONG.

WHAT ARE
THEY SAYING? I CAN'T
HEAR ANYTHING.

DON'T!

A FEW MINUTES TURNED INTO AN HOUR...
BOOGERS FOR FINGERS 24/7 OR FARTING FIFTY TIMES A DAY?
FARTING. THAT'S EASY!
BOOGER HANDS. I'D JUST WEAR WATERPROOF GLOVES.

IN THE SUMMER? BUT YOU'D BE ALL SWEATY.
WE LIVE IN IRELAND, REMEMBER?

THIS SUCKS.

WANT TO
PLAY "WOULD YOU
RATHER" AGAIN?
NO!

MAM!
OH NO!
AHH!

JUST SAY IT!
I'M GROUNDED FOREVER,
AREN'T I?
NO, YOU'RE
NOT GROUNDED.

WHAT
?!?

YOUR DAD WANTS TO
TALK TO YOU ABOUT SOMETHING
IMPORTANT. JUST BECAUSE WE'RE NOT
TOGETHER ANYMORE DOESN'T
MEAN YOU CAN'T SEE HIM
AND TALK TO HIM.

SWEAT WAS ROLLING DOWN HIS HEAD.

HIS HANDS KEEP MOVING, LIKE HE'S TRYING TO SHAKE WATER OFF THEM.

THAT'S THE BIGGEST BREATH I'VE EVER SEEN ANYONE TAKE!

REMEMBER WHEN I SAID I GOT BULLIED IN SCHOOL? PEOPLE THOUGHT I WAS WEIRD, TOO.
IT'S ONLY NOW THAT I'M OLDER, I'VE REALIZED A FEW THINGS.

LAST YEAR, I WAS DIAGNOSED WITH SOMETHING CALLED AUTISM.
WHAT THE HECK IS THAT?! CAN I CATCH IT FROM YOU?
ALL IT MEANS IS YOUR DAD'S BRAIN IS WIRED A LITTLE DIFFERENTLY.

SO... YOUR BRAIN'S BROKEN?
THE OPPOSITE, ACTUALLY. IT'S LIKE HAVING A DIFFERENT OPERATING SYSTEM. IT JUST WORKS IN ANOTHER WAY!

I FELT LIKE AN OUTSIDER FOR MOST OF MY LIFE UNTIL I REALIZED ONE DAY THAT IT DOESN'T MATTER WHAT PEOPLE THINK OF ME. IF THEY DON'T LIKE ME BECAUSE I'M A BIT DIFFERENT, THEN THAT'S THEIR LOSS.

I USED TO ALWAYS SAY THE WRONG THING AT THE WRONG TIME, TOO. I STILL DO SOMETIMES! AND THAT'S OK.
I ALSO FOUND IT HARD TO CONCENTRATE IN SCHOOL BECAUSE IT WAS TOO NOISY. DOES THAT EVER HAPPEN TO YOU?

EVERYTHING MY DAD SAID SOUNDED EXACTLY LIKE ME. I THOUGHT I WAS THE ONLY ONE LIKE THIS.

BOOM
I'D NEVER FELT ALL MY FEELINGS AT ONCE BEFORE.

SO YOU'RE REALLY NOT AN ALIEN?
I'M AFRAID NOT.
DOES THAT MEAN I'M NOT AN ALIEN, EITHER?

CAN WE GO HOME NOW? I'M REALLY TIRED.
I KNOW, YOU'VE HAD A LONG DAY. WE HAVE A LOT TO TALK ABOUT, BUT THERE'S NO HURRY.

I TOLD YOU NOT TO WEAR THAT TOP. IT LOOKS AWFUL.
WHAT IS SHE DOING HERE?

OH BOY!

THIS IS MY GIRLFRIEND, RACHEL!

BUT THAT'S HER MAM?

DOES THAT MEAN...
SHE'S MY SISTER?!! I DON'T WANT HER TO BE MY SISTER!

WELL, I DON'T WANT TO BE YOUR SISTER, EITHER.

MY WORST NIGHTMARE
CAN YOU IMAGINE...US, SISTERS?! I'D RATHER LISTEN TO POP MUSIC FOR THE REST OF MY LIFE!

WHY DOES HE HAVE TO GO OUT WITH HER? THERE'S LIKE A GAZILLION OTHER PEOPLE ON THE PLANET!
WELL, AT LEAST SHE DOESN'T LIVE THERE!
SAM'S RIGHT, YOU'LL NEVER SEE HER. IT WAS JUST UNFORTUNATE TONIGHT.

YEAH, LOOK AT THE POSITIVES! AT LEAST YOU KNOW YOU'RE NOT AN ALIEN AND CAN STAY ON PLANET EARTH WITH US!

WHERE WERE YOU TWO? DO YOU KNOW WHAT TIME IT IS?

IT WAS WEIRD SEEING MY DAD FOR THE FIRST TIME. MOST PEOPLE SEE THEIR DAD EVERY DAY!

I HAD THIS FUNNY FEELING IN MY STOMACH ALL DAY, AND AS SOON AS WE MET IT WENT AWAY!
I BELIEVE
IDLES
PUNK

I KNOW I'M NOT AN ALIEN NOW, BUT THAT DOESN'T MEAN I WOULDN'T LIKE TO GO ON A SPACESHIP...
FAMILY TRIP TO MARS

JUST A SHORT TRIP!

ANKIE'S ROOM
CAN I COME IN?

I'M SORRY, FRANKIE. I SHOULD HAVE TALKED TO YOU MORE ABOUT HOW YOU WERE FEELING. I JUST DIDN'T KNOW WHAT TO SAY.
IT'S OK, MAM. I LOVE YOU!

A LOT HAS CHANGED OVER THE LAST COUPLE OF MONTHS.

MY DAD'S TEACHING ME HOW TO PLAY THE GUITAR. SO NEXT TIME YOU SEE ME, I'M PROBABLY GOING TO BE FAMOUS!

HE'S STILL GOING OUT WITH NADINE'S MAM. I HAVEN'T SEEN THEM ALL SUMMER, THOUGH.

AND YOU'LL NEVER GUESS WHAT!
IT TURNS OUT I AM LIKE MY DAD!

AUTISM DIAGNOSIS
OK, A LOT LIKE MY DAD.

I TOLD SAM AND REBECCA, TOO.
IT MAKES SO MUCH SENSE WHEN YOU THINK ABOUT IT!
THAT'S AWESOME! CAN YOU SEE THROUGH COOKIE TINS?
WHAT? I HAVEN'T GOT MAGIC POWERS, REBECCA.

MY BRAIN

NOT "TOO SENSITIVE" OR BEING A "DRAMA QUEEN"

NEEDS A BREAK OR HOLIDAY SOMETIMES AND THAT'S OK

THE REASON I ONLY REALLY LIKE TO EAT FOUR THINGS: PIZZA, WAFFLES, EGGS, AND CHOCOLATE

IS ABLE TO HOLD ALL SORTS OF FACTS THAT I WILL PROBABLY NEVER NEED

NO WONDER MY BRAIN DIDN'T KNOW WHAT TO DO. IT HAD THE WRONG MANUAL.
FINALLY!
THE ULTIMATE GUIDE TO FRANKIE'S WORLD

NOW THAT I HAVE THE RIGHT ONE, THINGS HAVE NEVER BEEN BETTER.

I'M NOT PERFECT, NOBODY IS. BUT AT LEAST I'M ME!

I BELIEVE
IDLES
PUNK
FRANKIE! COME ON, WE'RE WAITING!
COMING, MAM!

SAY CHEESE!

ACKNOWLEDGMENTS

I would like to start by thanking my amazing editors Yasmin Morrissey and Ruth Bennett along with Lauren Fortune for their continuous support throughout working on *Frankie's World*. Your energy, encouragement, and patience have been next to none. It has been one of the most uplifting experiences of my life to work with such an epic group of people who are just as excited about *Frankie's World* as I am. I have felt that energy with every interaction and it means everything to me, so thank you.

To all the team at Scholastic who I have met virtually and those I have yet to meet, thank you for all the time and energy you have put into *Frankie's World* and helping to bring this book to life.

To Andrew Biscomb, Tracey Cunnell, and Rachel Lawston, for giving *Frankie's World* a magic touch and who with their expertise have taken this book beyond what I ever dreamed.

To Alex Hynes, for helping make the typeface for my book possible and always supporting from afar.

To Faith, my agent. Thank you for believing in me and supporting me through all my endeavors. You have been a driving force in my life and took a chance on me when not many people did. I thank you for your patience, kindness, and everything you have done for me since the day we first met.

To my partner, Karl, thank you so much for all of your support. You have gone above and beyond over the years (and that's an understatement) and have been by my side through absolutely everything. You are truly the most amazing person I have ever met.

To my friends Bonnie, Marisa, and Chris, for showing me what true friends really are and for accepting me for who I am. You always show up. Even when I least expect it.

To my mam and dad, who are not with me anymore, but I know are shining down on me every day.

To my sister Orla, my niece Calla, and to all my family for everything.

To my nana, for supporting me and being by my side through college and always cheering me on from the sidelines.

To Uncle Dan, for always walking to the shop with me and introducing me to a world of imagination and fun.

And finally, a special thanks to: Will McDermott, who gave me a chance in my college interview and years later would give me an old drawing tablet. You made such an impact in my life and I will be forever grateful for your kindness.

Marc Doyle, who encouraged me to draw even more after looking at my notebooks. "Aoife, this is your niche!" is what you said. I have never forgotten that day in the National Art Gallery.

Tom, John, and Con, my lecturers from DIT, for always keeping it real. Thank you for your continued support (even after college) and for all the fun memories.

WHAT IS AUTISM?

Autism is a complex, invisible condition that a person is born with. Autism is a developmental condition, which means that the way a person communicates, interacts, and understands other people and the world is different from those who do not have the condition. It can be described as a "spectrum," which means it impacts different people in different ways, to differing degrees, at different times and in different situations.

Autism is not a linear scale or line with people at one end being "mildly autistic" and experiencing few challenges in any area and then people at the other end being "severely affected" and experiencing all the challenges all the time. This does not reflect how people experience autism.

Thinking of autism as being a spectrum is a much more helpful and accurate concept to understand the variation and individuality across autistic people.

Autism is said to be a spectrum because while autistic people can experience the world differently in specific areas, like sensory processing and communication, not all people will have the same profile of differences. So, you could have one autistic person who enjoys public speaking and has a very strong preference for routine. But another autistic person could find spoken communication very challenging but quite enjoy going to new places with little preparation. The autism spectrum is a very wide one, with people affected in a variety of ways, to a great number of varying degrees, and no two people on the spectrum are affected in entirely the same way.

Text from ASIAM with kind permission.
Please visit ASIAM.IE for more information.

When talking about autism, it is as important to know what is not true as what is true about the condition. While autism awareness has greatly grown in recent years, we are still a long way from having a society that truly understands autism. Although many people have heard the word or even know someone with the condition, many people still cannot explain what autism is or understand the way autistic people think.

AUTISTIC PEOPLE LACK EMPATHY

This one always makes me giggle, and I know a lot of people on the spectrum can relate, but I think that we actually feel all the feels.

BUT YOU DON'T LOOK AUTISTIC?

"What does an autistic person look like?" is a question that doesn't acknowledge autism is invisible. It doesn't have a shape, size, or color.

AUTISTIC PEOPLE DON'T WANT FRIENDS

Most children want friends and to be included, and that is no different for autistic children.

AUTISTIC PEOPLE DON'T GET HUMOR

Sometimes a joke will go over my head, sure! But I love comedy and very much get most types of humor.

AUTISTIC PEOPLE ARE MATH GENIUSES

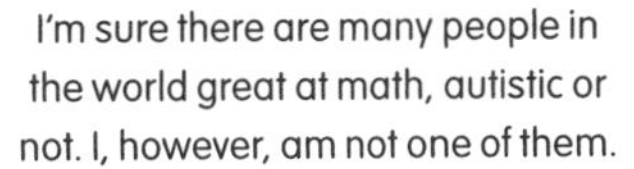

I'm sure there are many people in the world great at math, autistic or not. I, however, am not one of them.

AUTISTIC PEOPLE CAN'T...

Every person has abilities, including autistic people. We should never assume an autistic person can't do something, but rather talk about how we can empower autistic people to be able to participate.

HOW TO BE A GOOD FRIEND

There are many ways to be a good friend, like Sam and Rebecca are to Frankie. To me, a friend is someone who supports you, is there when times are tough, someone who listens, and most importantly, someone you can trust. I found it hard to make friends growing up, and sometimes it can be lonely when others don't really understand you. Below are some things I've learned along the way that have helped me to be a good friend, and to notice when someone is being a good friend to me. It costs nothing to be kind and you might just make someone else's day.

A REAL FRIEND SUPPORTS YOU AND CHEERS YOU ON.

I LIKE TO TREAT OTHERS THE WAY I LIKE TO BE TREATED.

DON'T STAND BY WHEN SOMEONE IS BEING BULLIED. STAND UP AND SPEAK OUT. YOU COULD REALLY HELP SOMEONE.

A REAL FRIEND IS SOMEONE WHO LISTENS AND WANTS TO HELP BECAUSE THEY CARE.

REAL FRIENDS ACCEPT YOU FOR WHO YOU ARE.

WHAT'S YOUR SUPERHERO NAME?

PICK THE MONTH YOU WERE BORN AND THE FIRST LETTER OF YOUR NAME TO FIND OUT YOUR FUNNY SUPERHERO NAME!

JAN **Captain**
FEB **Turbo**
MAR **Magic**
APR **Danger**
MAY **Galactic**
JUN **Doctor**
JUL **Supersonic**
AUG **Epic**
SEP **Mystical**
OCT **Crystal**
NOV **Cosmo**
DEC **Frightening**

A **Barnacle**
B **Storm Slayer**
C **Lightning Strike**
D **Broccoli Beam**
E **Banana**
F **Wonder Wizard**
G **Star Shooter**
H **Space Pizza**
I **Thunder Beam**
J **Waffles**
K **Thunder Fart**
L **Hot Dog**
M **Nugget Ninja**

N **Brain Storm**
O **Space Doughnut**
P **Justice Juice**
Q **Iron Shadow**
R **Cookie Slayer**
S **Rainbow Ray**
T **Illusion**
U **Sprinkles**
V **Steel Arm**
W **Milk Menace**
X **Space Slayer**
Y **Waffle Warrior**
Z **Ice Blaster**

NOTES
(LOTS OF NOTES)
DOODLES
SLAM
DUNK

ABOUT THE AUTHOR

AOIFE DOOLEY is an award-winning comedian, writer, and illustrator from Dublin. She's the creator of a counting board book, *1 2 3 Ireland!*, which won an Irish Book Award. She is also the creator and animator of *Your One Nikita*, a web series of TV shorts that has a loyal online fan base. Aoife openly shares her experiences of being diagnosed with autism at the age of twenty-seven and how her diagnosis has helped her to truly understand herself. Visit Aoife online at aoifedooleydesign.com.

YEAH
OOPS